Donated by
Editorial Directions
in honor of
The Koutris Family
to the
Olive-Mary Stitt LMC
2003-2004

OUR GALAXY AND BEYOND

EARTH

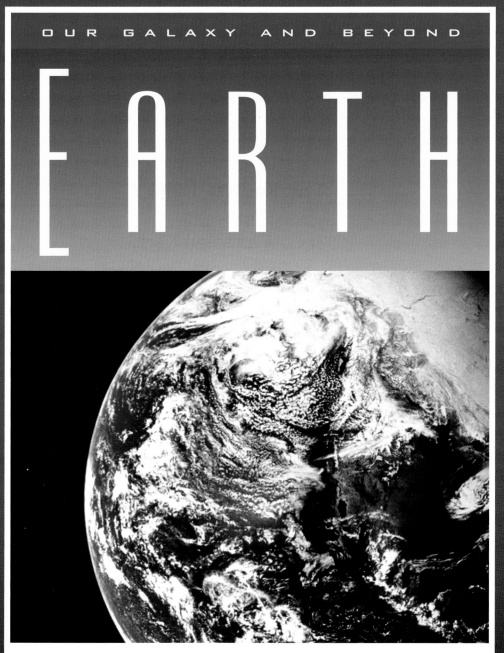

By Darlene R. Stille

THE CHILD'S WORLD®

CHANHASSEN, MINNESOTA

The Child's World

Published in the United States of America by The Child's World®
P.O. Box 326, Chanhassen, MN 55317-0326
800-599-READ
www.childsworld.com

Content Adviser:
Michelle Nichols,
Lead Educator for
Informal Programs,
Adler Planetarium
& Astronomy
Museum, Chicago,
Illinois

Photo Credits: Cover: NASA/Ames Research Center; Corbis: 5 (James Randklev), 6 (Archivo Iconografico, S. A.), 7 (Bettmann), 8 (NASA/Roger Ressmeyer), 10 (Stefano Bianchetti), 11 (Shepard Sherbell/Corbis Saba), 16, 22 (Cindy Kassab), 25 (Sally A. Morgan; Ecoscene), 27 (Gary Braasch); F. Hasler/M. Jentoft-Nilsen/H. Pierce/K. Palaniappan/M. Manyin/NASA Goddard Lab for Atmosphere: 15; NASA/GSFC/LaRC/JPL, MISR Team: 9, 14; NASA/GSFC/METI/ERSDAC/JAROS/U.S.-Japan ASTER Science Team: 12, 20, 23; NASA/JPL/Caltech: 18, 19, 31; NASA/JPL/Caltech/NIMA: 24.

The Child's World®: Mary Berendes, Publishing Director
Editorial Directions, Inc.: E. Russell Primm, Editorial Director; Dana Rau, Line Editor; Elizabeth K. Martin, Assistant Editor; Olivia Nellums, Editorial Assistant; Susan Hindman, Copy Editor; Susan Ashley, Proofreader; Kevin Cunningham, Peter Garnham, Chris Simms, Fact Checkers; Tim Griffin/IndexServ, Indexer; Cian Loughlin O'Day, Photo Researcher; Linda S. Koutris, Photo Selector

Library of Congress Cataloging-in-Publication Data
Stille, Darlene R.
  Earth / by Darlene Stille.
    p. cm. — (Our galaxy and beyond)
Summary: Introduces Earth as a planet, exploring its atmosphere, composition, and other characteristics and looking particularly at how humans learned about the blue-green ball on which we live. Includes bibliographical references and index.
  ISBN 1-59296-048-0 (lib. bdg. : alk. paper)
  1. Earth—Juvenile literature. [1. Earth.] I. Title. II. Series.
  QB631.4.S744 2004
  525—dc21   2003006330

TABLE OF CONTENTS

CHAPTER ONE

DISCOVERING EARTH

When you think of Earth, you probably think of mountains, oceans, forests, lakes, and rivers. But do you ever think about Earth as a planet in space? We know more about Earth than any other planet, because we live on Earth.

What if you were a visitor from somewhere else in space? How would Earth look to you? Astronauts have looked down on their planet from their spacecraft. They saw a blue-green ball turning in the blackness of space. They saw white clouds swirling above the ball. They saw a planet that orbits, or goes around, a star.

Earth is one of nine planets orbiting a star we call the Sun. The Sun and the planets are called the solar system. Earth is the fifth largest planet in our solar system. Its diameter, the distance from one

Though Earth is similar to the other rocky planets, Mercury, Venus, and Mars, it has one major difference: Earth is rich with life. Many different kinds of plants and animals live in the Kalalau Valley in Hawaii.

side of the planet to the other, is 7,926.41 miles (12,756.32 kilometers). Earth is also the third planet from the Sun. It orbits the Sun in a path that is almost a circle, but not quite. This means that it is not always the same distance away from the Sun.

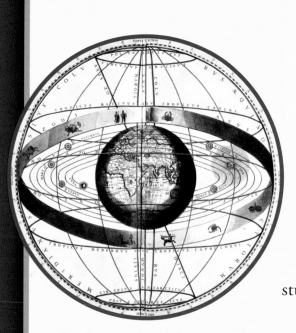

People once believed that Earth was the center of the universe, as this old map shows.

It took people a long time to learn about Earth. People who lived long ago could not travel very far. They had to walk or ride on animals. They studied the sky, but they could not see very far into space. Some people thought Earth was flat. They worried that if they traveled too far, they might fall off Earth's edge.

The ancient Greeks tried to understand Earth's place in the sky. The Greeks called the Sun, Moon, stars, and planets "spheres." A sphere is round like a ball. Greek **astronomers** thought all the spheres in the sky went around Earth. For a long time, people thought that Earth was the center of the universe.

After the **telescope** was invented in 1608, astronomers

Han Lippershey was an eyeglass maker who is credited with inventing the telescope.

could study the spheres better. By the 1600s, astronomers had dis-

covered that Earth and the other planets orbit the Sun. Only the

Moon orbits Earth. They discovered that our star is one of millions

of stars in our galaxy, called the Milky Way. A galaxy is a huge group

of stars, planets, gases, and dust held together by forces of gravity.

Early astronomers also learned that the Milky Way is one of millions

of galaxies in the universe.

When the northern part of Earth is tipped toward the Sun, as in this picture, that half of the world experiences summer. At the same time, it will be winter in the southern part of Earth.

The telescope helped these early scientists learn more about how Earth travels in the solar system. Earth spins on its axis as it orbits the Sun. Earth's axis is like an imaginary stick going through the center of the planet. As Earth turns, part of the planet gets light from the Sun and part of it is in darkness. We have day and night because Earth turns. This turning also makes the stars seem to move across the sky.

Each trip that Earth makes around the Sun is one year. During the year, there are four seasons in the northern and southern halves of Earth. Spring, summer, autumn, and winter are the seasons. We have seasons because Earth is tilted on its axis as it goes around the Sun. When the northern half is tipped toward the Sun, it is summer in the northern half and winter in the southern half. When the southern half is tipped toward the Sun, it is winter in the north and summer in the south.

A snowstorm moves across the eastern United States as the northern part of Earth tilts away from the Sun and winter arrives.

No one knows when the first people began to explore Earth. Scientists think the first explorers were **prehistoric** people who left Africa and traveled north. Thousands of years ago, people left Asia and moved to North America. They became the Native Americans. The ancient Chinese, people from the Middle East, and the ancient Greeks all explored parts of the world.

In the 1400s, Europeans set out in ships to find out what was beyond the Atlantic and Pacific Oceans. They landed on the continents of North and South America. They sailed around Africa. In 1517, the crew of Portuguese **navigator** Ferdinand Magellan became the first explorers to sail completely around the world. Magellan himself died in the Philippines before he could complete this journey. Explorers discovered the continent of Antarctica, near the South Pole, in the 1800s.

By the 1900s, scientists had taken over the job of exploring Earth. They measured the heights of mountains. They dove into the deepest parts of the ocean. They studied the many forms of life all over the world. They made the first maps of the entire planet. They launched satellites to study Earth. Satellites orbit the Earth and take pictures, do tests, and take measurements. All of these studies have given scientists a good idea of what Earth is like.

CHAPTER TWO

EARTH'S ATMOSPHERE

Earth is surrounded by a layer of gases called the atmosphere. We call the gases in Earth's atmosphere "air." The air we breathe contains several gases. The gas most important to us is oxygen. All animals must breathe in oxygen to live.

Scientists in Sweden launch a weather balloon to measure the ozone levels in the Arctic.

The Thames River comes into view as NASA does research from space to track London's pollution levels and population growth.

Scientists think Earth's atmosphere changed over time. When the atmosphere first formed, it was mostly carbon dioxide. There was very little oxygen. Chemical changes sent much of the carbon dioxide into the oceans, rocks, and plants. Plants made oxygen and sent it into the atmosphere.

Today, oxygen is about 21 percent of Earth's atmosphere. Nitrogen is about 78 percent. Small amounts of carbon dioxide and other gases make up about 1 percent. There is also a layer of a gas called ozone in the atmosphere. Ozone blocks harmful rays from the Sun that can cause skin cancer. Some types of pollution have made holes in the ozone layer. The holes are near the North and South Poles.

Earth's atmosphere goes up from the surface of the planet for about 600 miles (1,000 km). The higher you go, the thinner the air gets. Planes flying in Earth's atmosphere must carry their own air, because there is so little oxygen in the high atmosphere.

The atmosphere causes weather on Earth. Parts of the atmosphere can be hot or cold at different times of the year. Winds blow in the atmosphere. Clouds form in the part of the atmosphere closest to Earth. Rain and snow come down from the clouds.

THE GREENHOUSE EFFECT

Have you ever been inside a greenhouse? A greenhouse has glass walls and a glass roof. It stays warm enough for plants to grow even if it is cold outside. The glass traps heat from the Sun. Carbon dioxide acts like the glass roof and walls of a greenhouse. Without carbon dioxide in the atmosphere, Earth would be too cold for life. But with too much carbon dioxide in the atmosphere, Earth would be too hot for life. Earth's atmosphere is

But humans may be changing that perfect atmosphere. Many scientists believe that people are putting too much carbon dioxide into the atmosphere. Carbon dioxide is in smoke from factories and in the exhaust from cars. Too much carbon dioxide would trap too much heat from the Sun. This is called the runaway greenhouse effect. It would make Earth warmer. It could change the weather on Earth. It could melt the ice caps and

CHAPTER THREE

WHAT EARTH IS MADE OF

No other planet in the solar system looks like Earth. The surface

of Earth is part land and part water. In fact, 71 percent of the planet is

covered with water. Some of the water is salt water. Salt water fills the

*This view from space of the Pacific Ocean gives a good idea of just
how much of Earth is covered with saltwater.*

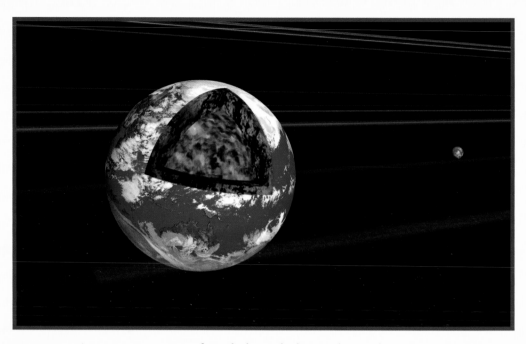

A cross-section image of Earth shows the hot, molten rock at its center.

oceans. Water that does not contain salt is called freshwater.

Freshwater fills lakes and rivers. Earth is the only planet in the solar

system that has liquid water on its surface. Earth also has frozen water,

or ice. There is always ice at the North and South Poles.

The land areas of Earth are called continents and islands.

Continents are big land areas, while islands are small land areas.

Continents and islands rise up much higher than the seafloor.

The seafloor is under the water of the ocean. The land areas of Earth have high mountains and flat plains. Some of the mountains are **volcanoes.** Hot melted rock from inside the Earth erupts out of the volcanoes.

Earth is like a ball made up of different layers. The outer layer is called the crust. It is made of rocks and soil. Below the crust is a layer called the mantle. The mantle is made of hot, melted rock. The center of Earth is called the core. It is made mostly of iron. The outer layer of the core is melted iron. The inner core is solid iron. Strange as it seems, the different layers of Earth spin around Earth's axis separately. The inner core spins faster than the crust and mantle.

Scientists think that liquid iron moving around in the core gives Earth a magnetic field. A magnetic field is the area around a magnet where its pull can be felt.

Earth has only one moon. The Moon is the only place in the solar system that people have visited. Astronauts went to the Moon on the *Apollo* space-craft. The first astronauts land-ed on the Moon in 1969. The United States and the Soviet Union (now Russia) also sent many unmanned spacecraft to study the Moon. Unmanned spacecraft do not have peo-ple aboard.

The Moon is made of gray rocks and soil. It has both smooth plains and rugged mountains. Its surface is cov-ered with craters. Some craters were made by meteorites strik-ing the Moon. Some craters look like the tops of volcanoes.

Scientists think that melted rock from volcanoes made the plains on the Moon. The Moon does not shine. The moonlight that we see from Earth is really just sunlight bouncing off the Moon.

Scientists have different ideas about where the Moon came from. One idea is that a Mars-sized **comet** slammed into Earth billions of years ago. The crash sent chunks of rock into space around Earth. The chunks came together to form the Moon. Rocks that astronauts found on the Moon are a lot like rocks on Earth. But scientists still need to do more studies to understand how the Moon came to be.

CHAPTER FOUR

THE JIGSAW PUZZLE OF EARTH

In the mid-1900s, scientists came up with an idea about Earth's

crust called plate tectonics. This idea explains why volcanoes erupt and

how mountains form. According to the idea of plate tectonics, the

crust of Earth is like a jigsaw puzzle. It is made of about 30 pieces

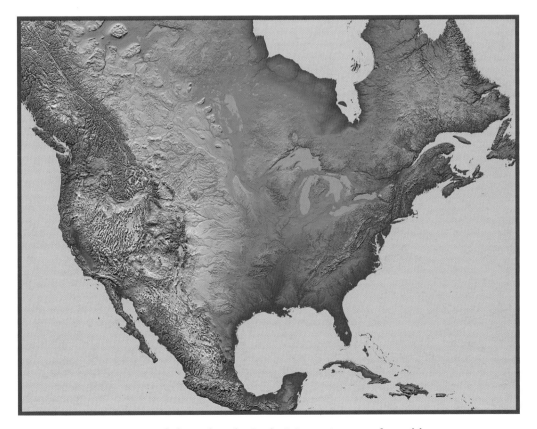

*Scientists believe that the Rocky Mountains were formed by
tectonic plates crashing together beneath Earth's surface.*

called plates. The plates slide around slowly on the melted rock in the mantle. Some plates move toward each other. Some plates move away from one another. Some plates slide past each other.

Plates moving toward each other sometimes crunch together. The edges of the plates fold up to form mountain ranges. Sometimes, one plate slips under the plate it is moving toward and goes down into the hot mantle, where it melts. The melted rock comes up through the crust of Earth and makes a volcano.

Plates moving away from each other make up part of the seafloor. As they move apart, they leave cracks in the crust. Melted rock from the mantle oozes up in the cracks. The melted rock cools and hardens to make new crust.

Plates that slide past one another or crash into each other cause the ground to shake violently. This is called an earthquake.

This image from space shows Mount Etna in Italy during an eruption as lava flows toward the town of Nicolosi.

Earthquakes make waves. These waves are like waves that travel through water. But earthquake waves travel through rock! Earthquake waves are sometimes strong enough to knock down buildings. Many, though, are too weak to be felt by people. Scientists study these waves to learn what it is like inside Earth.

CHAPTER FIVE

THE CHANGING EARTH

The surface of Earth also changes in other ways. Three things cause these changes: weathering, erosion, and mass movements. Weathering is the breaking up of rocks. Water gets into cracks in rocks. When it freezes, water expands and breaks the rock. Rocks can also dissolve in water. Sand comes from a type of rock called granite that dissolves and crumbles into tiny grains.

Erosion is the movement of soil and rocks from one place to another. Wind can blow soil from farmland. Rushing water can carry away the

As waves crash against rocks year after year, the rocks are worn down and their shapes change.

This three-dimensional image shows the vertical drop from the top of the Grand Canyon to the bottom. In some areas, the Grand Canyon is as much as 5,000 feet (1,525 m) deep.

banks of a river, leaving a canyon. Waves of water on lakeshores and

seashores can change the shape of the land. Huge rivers of ice, called

glaciers, also cause erosion. When glaciers move forward, they grind

up rock and push it into piles. When glaciers melt, they leave piles of

rock and soil behind. Until about 11,000 years ago, glaciers covered

much of North America. These glaciers carved out five deep holes.

After the glaciers melted, the holes filled with water and became the

Great Lakes.

Mass movement is the sudden movement of big sections of Earth. Landslides and mudslides occur when rocks and earth or mud suddenly slide down a mountain. Earthquakes are the biggest mass movements. Mass movements change the surface of Earth very quickly, while weathering and erosion take many years. All of these kinds of changes have shaped the way that Earth looks today.

The mountains surrounding Los Angeles are still forming. The plates beneath them do a lot of shifting and moving, which causes earthquakes.

LIFE ON EARTH

There are plants and animals living almost everywhere on Earth. They can live in deep oceans or on grassy plains. Life exists in some of the hottest deserts and on some of the coldest mountaintops. Earth is the only planet known to have life. One reason for life on Earth is water. All types of life we know of need water to live. The other reason for life is that Earth has oxygen and just the right amount of carbon dioxide in its atmosphere.

Scientists study fossils to Fossils are bones, shells, or other signs of dead plants or animals left in rock. Scientists look for clues that may tell them when life began. They think that life began on Earth about 3.5 billion years ago. The first living things may have been in the oceans. They may have been tiny **organisms** too small to see with just our eyes. The first living things on land may have been simple plants. Plants gave off oxygen. When there was enough oxygen in the atmosphere, animal

CHAPTER SIX

HOW EARTH
MAY HAVE FORMED

The Sun, Earth, and other planets probably formed about 4.6 billion years ago. They may have formed from a hot cloud of dust and gas swirling in space. That cloud flattened into a spinning disk. In the part of the disk closest to the Sun, small, rocky planets formed. One of these planets was Earth.

Earth may have started as a spinning ball of rock and metal. Slowly, the ball grew hotter and melted. Heavy iron sank to the center of the ball. Lighter rocks floated to the surface. Earth's atmosphere may have formed from material from comets or **asteroids** that crashed into Earth. The atmosphere may have also been formed by volcanic eruptions. These eruptions could have been a source of water for the oceans. At one time, water formed one big ocean on Earth.

Geologists, or scientists who study rocks, think that at one time, Earth had one big continent. The continent broke into two pieces. The two continents sat on plates that make up Earth's crust. The plates moved away from each other. The

Geologists carry equipment up the side of Mount Saint Helens, in Washington, to record changes that have taken place at its top.

two continents broke into the seven continents that we know today.

Scientists still have many questions about Earth. One of these questions is how Earth and the other planets of our solar system formed. They hope that their knowledge of Earth will help them learn more about how other planets work. And they hope that studying other planets may help them answer some of those remaining questions about our own.

Glossary

asteroids (ASS-tuh-royds) Asteroids are rocky objects that orbit the Sun.

astronomers (uh-STRAW-nuh-merz) Astronomers are scientists who study space and the stars and planets.

comet (KOM-it) A comet is a bright object followed by a tail of dust and ice that orbits the Sun in a long, oval-shaped path.

navigator (NAV-uh-gate-uhr) A navigator is a person who directs how to get somewhere, using maps, instruments, or even the stars as guides.

organisms (OR-guh-niz-uhmz) Organisms are living things, such as plants or animals.

prehistoric (pree-hiss-TOR-ik) Something that is prehistoric is very old, from the time before history was first recorded.

telescope (TEL-uh-skope) A telescope is an instrument used to study things that are far away, such as stars and planets, by making them seem larger and closer.

volcanoes (vol-KAY-nose) Volcanoes are mountains that contain an opening in Earth's surface. When a volcano erupts, melted rock from pools of magma below the surface spews from the top.

Did You Know?

▶ Earth looks like a round ball, but it is shaped more like a pear. Earth is flattened at the North and South Poles and bulges out slightly just south of its equator, the imaginary line around the middle of the planet.

▶ It is very hot deep inside Earth. The mantle can be as hot as 8,000° F (4,400° C). The inner part of the core may be 13,000° F (7,000° C). That is hotter than the surface of the Sun!

▶ Gravity is what holds you down on Earth. Gravity is a force that pulls one object toward another. Gravity holds the Moon in orbit around Earth and Earth in orbit around the Sun.

▶ Earth's crust is thinner under the oceans and thicker under the continents. The crust is an average of 4 miles (7 km) thick under the oceans and 25 miles (40 km) thick under the continents.

▶ The deepest part of the ocean is the Mariana Trench in the Pacific Ocean. It is 36,198 feet (11,033 m) below the surface of the water. Earth's highest mountain is Mount Everest in Asia. It rises 29,028 feet (8,848 m) above the level of the sea.

Fast Facts

Diameter: 7,926.41 miles (12,756.32 km)

Atmosphere: nitrogen, oxygen, argon, carbon dioxide

Time to orbit the Sun (one Earth-year): 365 days, 6 hours, 9, minutes, 9.54 seconds

Time to turn on axis (one Earth-day): 23 hours, 56 minutes, 4.091 seconds (one day)

Average distance from the Sun: about 93 million miles (150 million km)

Shortest distance from the Sun: 91 million miles (146 million km)

Greatest distance from the Sun: 94.5 million miles (152 million km)

Temperature range: 136° F (58° C) to –128.6° F (–89.2° C)

Number of known moons: 1

How to Learn More about Earth

At the Library

Friend, Sandra. *Earth's Wild Winds.*
Brookfield, Conn.: Twenty-First Century Books, 2002.

Margaret, Amy, and Luke Thompson. *Earth.*
New York: Powerkids, 2001.

Marzollo, Jean, and Judith Moffatt (illustrator). *I am Planet Earth.*
New York: Scholastic, 2000.

Simon, Seymour. *Earth: Our Planet in Space.*
New York: Simon and Schuster Books for Young Readers, 2003.

Smiley, Simon. *E.T. the Extra Terrestrial Discovers Planet Earth.*
New York: Kingfisher/Universal, 2002.

On the Web

Visit our home page for lots of links about Earth:
http://www.childsworld.com/links.html
Note to Parents, Teachers, and Librarians: We routinely verify our Web links to
make sure they're safe, active sites—so encourage your readers to check them out!

Through the Mail or by Phone

ROSE CENTER FOR EARTH AND SPACE
AMERICAN MUSEUM OF NATURAL HISTORY
Central Park West at 79th Street
New York, NY 10024-5192
212/769-5100

U.S. GEOLOGICAL SURVEY
509 National Center
Reston, VA 20192
703/648-4748

The solar system

Index

About the Author

Darlene R. Stille is a science writer. She has lived in Chicago, Illinois, all her life. When she was in high school, she fell in love with science. While attending the University of Illinois she discovered that she also loved writing. She was fortunate to find a career that allowed her to combine both her interests. Darlene Stille has written about 60 books for young people.